Enid Blyton's™

The Valley of
Adventure

Screenplay novelisation by
Andrew Donkin

Collins
An imprint of HarperCollinsPublishers

Original screenplay by
Harry Duffin.

This screenplay novelisation first published
in Great Britain by Collins 1997
1 3 5 7 9 10 8 6 4 2

Collins is an imprint of HarperCollins*Publishers* Ltd,
77-85 Fulham Palace Road, Hammersmith, London W6 8JB.

Copyright © Enid Blyton Ltd 1997

ISBN 0 00 675312 4

The author asserts the moral right to be
identified as the author of this work.

Printed and bound in Great Britain by
Caledonian International Book Manufacturing Ltd,
Glasgow, G64

The Valley of Adventure

Torrential rain beat against the entrance to the cave.

"If it keeps on like this, it'll wash the whole cave away," said Dinah.

The biggest lightning flash yet exploded and there was another thunderous roar, but for once it wasn't the weather. Pieces of rock began to fall down on the three children.

Philip pushed the girls deeper into the cavern. Behind them, a large boulder crashed down near the entrance. Lucy-Ann screamed.

"It's gone totally dark," she cried, reaching in her rucksack for her torch. She shone it towards the entrance.

It was completely blocked by fallen rock.

"We're trapped," said Dinah softly. "Buried underground."

*There are eight screenplay novelisations
starring Philip, Dinah, Jack and Lucy-Ann from the
Channel Five Enid Blyton™ Adventure Series:*

*All published by
HarperCollinsPublishers Ltd*

CHAPTER ONE

The old man looked haunted as he made his way along the street, his tired, worn-out feet scraping along the pavement. He slowed down even further outside a restaurant window, and finally came to a halt. With a look of hunger on his aged face, he gazed at the customers eating their evening meals.

For a second, Otto Sheer's own reflection in the restaurant window caught his attention, then he moved on, unaware that he was being followed by another man of similar age, Father Paul.

The priest looked across the street after watching Otto for a few more minutes, then nodded to two tough-looking men sitting in a parked van nearby.

"That's it. That must be him," said Terry.

Terry Small was an East End wide boy and villain for hire. At his side, Ivan, a huge bear-like Russian, nodded in agreement.

Otto had now turned a corner into a side street. Suddenly the van came skidding to a halt by his side and Terry leapt out.

"Are you Otto? Otto Scheer?" said Terry, brandishing a large gun.

The old man reacted to the unexpected sound of his name.

"Get in!" smiled Terry, satisfied that this was his target.

"Help me! Someone, help!" cried Otto, as Terry grabbed him and dragged him towards the back of the van.

Terry saw a nearby policeman change his course to investigate and quickly bundled Otto into the back of the van. Then he spun round and raised his gun.

"Back off, copper!" he shouted.

The policeman dived for cover. Terry raced round to the front of the van.

"Go! Go!" he said, jumping back inside.

The van roared away. The policeman just had time to see its registration number before it skidded round the corner and was gone.

Otto Scheer had just been kidnapped.

At Craggy Tops, Jack was in extreme danger of going deaf. His parrot, Kiki, was practising her loudest impression of a police car siren.

"Kiki! Be quiet," pleaded Jack.

"Mealtimes never used to be this noisy," said Alison Mannering, looking round at the children seated at her kitchen table. On her left sat her own two children, Dinah and Philip, and on the other side of the table were Lucy-Ann and her brother Jack, who was the owner of the unwanted police siren, Kiki, a parrot. Lucy-Ann and Jack Trent were best friends with Philip and Dinah, and usually lived with them in the holidays as their own parents had been killed in a car accident when they were very small.

"Good morning! Good morning!" said Kiki, jumping onto her perch.

"It's not morning, Kiki. It's nine o'clock in the evening," corrected Lucy-Ann, smiling.

Sitting on the opposite side of the table

was Bill Cunningham, a friend of Alison and her extended family. He worked for the Foreign Office and was the source of many of the children's adventures.

"Are we still going to fly tonight, Uncle Bill?" asked Philip.

"If the weather holds," said Bill.

"I heard a radio weather warning forecasting storms later," said Alison, concerned.

"Can your little plane fly in a storm, Uncle Bill?" asked Lucy-Ann.

"It can, but it's not much fun," said Bill.

Dinah put down her knife and fork. She was the last one to finish supper. "We'd better hurry up with the rest of the packing then," she said. The four children got up from the kitchen table.

"Don't pack too much," said Alison, raising her voice over the sound of moving chairs. "It's only a weekend."

"We'll need all our survival gear if we're going on a proper hike," said Jack, scooping Kiki up from her perch.

The children headed upstairs.

"And don't forget your sleeping bags,"

called Bill as they left. "It's at least one overcoat colder in Scotland at this time of the year."

The children spent an hour packing and they still weren't ready at the end of it. The bedroom floor was covered with half-packed rucksacks and sleeping bags, and right in the middle was Dinah, ticking off items on her list. "Food, boots, matches, torches."

Lucy-Ann held up her pencil torch proudly. "I've got mine."

"That's pathetic," sneered Jack.

"It's not as pathetic as you!" responded Lucy-Ann.

"Oh, and distress flares," said Dinah, finishing her list.

"Don't go mad, Di," said Philip. "It's only a weekend."

"You can never tell," said Dinah. "Whenever Uncle Bill's around something interesting always happens."

Kiki, meanwhile, had made her way inside one of the rucksacks, looking for something to eat. She had found some sandwiches, but her pecking noises alerted Lucy-Ann.

"Hey! Don't eat all the food before we get there, " she said.

"Poor Kiki! Poor Kiki!" said the disappointed parrot.

The children laughed and finished packing. When they were done, they climbed into the Land Rover and threw their rucksacks into the back. Kiki was with Jack in her travelling cage. She never liked that, but for Jack it was better than having her fly off at unexpected moments.

They set off for the airfield. It was already a windy night, but it seemed to be getting worse. Alison watched the weather worriedly – she didn't want to fly in a storm.

As they pulled into Ashburnham Airfield, they saw a large aircraft just warming up on the runway.

"I spy with my little eye something beginning with A," said Jack with a smile.

"Aeroplane!" shouted everybody in the Land Rover together. "Easiest clue in the world."

"Here we are, troops," announced Alison as they drove up to one of the airfield buildings. Bill's eight-seater plane was parked nearby, ready and waiting to take off.

"I need to go and file my flight plan," said Bill, getting out of the Land Rover.

"OK, I'll get the luggage on board and make sure everyone's settled down," said Alison.

"And don't forget those sleeping bags. It's going to be cold up in Scotland tonight," called Bill as he headed into the control tower.

The children grabbed their luggage and clambered excitedly out of the Land Rover. They glanced uneasily at the sky as a loud thunderclap sounded through the night sky.

"This is going to be great," said Philip, looking up at the dark mass of cloud above him.

"Stand by for take off!" said Kiki, in her most formal squawk.

On the other side of the airfield, the white van containing Terry, Ivan and the kidnapped Otto was making its way along

13

the perimeter fence. Otto was in the rear of the van trapped in a wicker basket filled with theatre costumes. Ivan was driving.

Terry hadn't stopped talking since they'd left the city, and Ivan was getting fed up with it.

"We won't be able to use the ferry now that copper got our registration number. They'll be watching the ports for us," he said.

"So what do we do?" asked Ivan.

"Just keep driving and trust your Uncle Terry," came the smug reply.

"You are not my uncle," said Ivan, sounding irritable.

"Well, you'd better trust me anyway. I'm all you've got, Boris, old mate," said Terry with a grin.

"My name is Ivan. Not Boris," complained Ivan.

There was a series of loud grunts from where Otto was trapped in the back of the van. Terry climbed into the rear and opened up the hamper.

"Help! Let me out!" said Otto indignantly. Terry looked around. He grabbed the top of a chicken costume and shoved it down on to Otto's head.

"Keep your beak shut!" he said, taking a second to admire his handiwork. Then he slammed the lid of the hamper shut and returned to his seat.

"Is this what we're looking for?" asked Ivan anxiously.

In front of them, the van's headlights illuminated a sign: Welcome to Ashburnham Airfield – Authorised Personnel Only it said.

"Here we are. Yup, this is it," said Terry.

"An aeroplane? I no understand," said the confused Ivan. "We're going to steal an aeroplane?"

"Some call it stealing," grinned Terry. "Me, I call it initiative. Let's go."

CHAPTER TWO

The children threw their rucksacks on board the plane and climbed in.

"It's brilliant!" said Lucy-Ann.

"Bill's so cool," said Dinah. "Only he would have his own plane!"

"Can I sit in the co-pilot's seat?" asked Philip, realising that one of them could sit next to Bill during the flight.

"I want to," said Jack, quickly.

"Now I don't want any arguments..." began Alison.

"There's nothing to see anyway. It's pitch black," said Dinah.

"How can Uncle Bill see to fly?" said Lucy-Ann, suddenly worried.

"With instruments," said Jack.

"Yeah, the trombone," said Philip, laughing.

"The trumpet."

"Saxophone."

"Bagpipes!"

"I hope you're not going to be like this all the way to Scotland," said Dinah, giving Philip and Jack a withering look.

Lucy-Ann put her head out of the door to talk to Alison. "It's getting really windy, isn't it? What do you think's keeping Bill?"

"I don't know, Lucy-Ann. I'll go and see," said Alison, walking away towards the tall high-tech building that was home to the airfield's control tower.

Inside, Bill was on the losing side of an argument with the Duty Controller.

"I'm sorry, but the weather is closing in just too fast," the Controller was explaining.

"There's still a window of clear weather before the storm," argued Bill.

"But it's getting smaller all the time and I'm not going to let you risk it," said the Controller firmly.

Alison walked inside and came up behind Bill.

"What's the matter, Bill?" said Alison,

realising immediately that there was a problem.

"I can't allow any more aircraft to take off tonight," said the Controller, answering Alison's question.

Bill tried one last personal appeal: "Look, I wouldn't fly if it wasn't safe. I'm a very experienced pilot," he said.

"I'm sorry. It's my responsibility and I think it's too risky." The Controller turned back to her radar screen, indicating that as far as she was concerned the matter was closed.

The children were sitting in the rear of the plane anxiously awaiting Bill's return so the flight could begin. They watched with surprise as Terry's white van raced in and skidded to a halt by the side of the aircraft.

"Who's this?" said Philip, peering out as the three men approached the plane.

"Bill didn't say there was anyone else coming on the trip," said Dinah, rather indignantly.

As the figures got nearer, they could see that one of them was being forced along at

18

gunpoint.

"That man's got a gun!" shrieked Lucy-Ann.

"Quickly, get out of sight and hide!" said Jack as the men headed for the door of the plane. The children quickly threw their sleeping bags over themselves and lay quite still just as Terry opened the door and pushed Otto on board. From where they were in the front of the plane, it looked quite empty.

"Move it, Fritz," urged Terry. "Sit down over there and shut up!"

"What are we going to do?" whispered Lucy-Ann, hidden under her sleeping bag.

"Keep very quiet," Jack whispered back.

Terry sat down in the pilot's seat right on top of a pair of binoculars.

"Ow!"

Ivan clambered into the co-pilot's seat next to him.

"You fly?" asked Ivan.

Terry looked down at the complicated controls in front of him.

"Hang about."

For a second he seemed totally lost.

"You do know how to fly?" repeated Ivan, growing more concerned.

Terry flicked the controls into life.

"'Course I can fly," he said, revving up the engine. "Just never bothered to get my licence, that's all."

Ivan closed his eyes in terror.

"He's going to take off!" whispered Philip frantically from the rear of the craft.

The plane jerked into motion.

"Right, gentlemen, hold on to your hats. Here we go. The maiden flight of Terry Small's Airlines," announced Terry proudly as the plane moved away.

Inside the control tower Alison heard the plane's engines come to life. She stared outside into the dark and saw the plane moving along the runway.

"Bill! The plane's started up! It's moving!" shouted Alison.

"What?!"

Bill and Alison ran out of the control tower. The Controller switched on a red flashlight and aimed it towards the departing plane.

Bill caught a glimpse of the two adult figures at the controls, but then the plane began moving away too fast for him to catch it. He dashed to the Land Rover and gave chase. The vehicle skidded off along the tarmac in pursuit of the escaping plane.

Terry was turning the plane ready for take off when Ivan spotted Bill driving towards them.

"Look!" he shouted.

Terry picked up speed in the plane, but Bill's Land Rover was coming ever closer.

"Aye, aye. Here we go. Chocks away, old son," said Terry, quite enjoying the chase.

Bill closed in on the plane but at the last moment Terry jerked up the flight controls and the plane skimmed over the roof of the Land Rover.

"Whoo! That was close," said Terry with a smile.

There was a sudden lightning flash in the sky around the plane followed by an ominous crack of thunder. The children groaned and looked at each other with anxious eyes as the plane hit turbulence. It rocked up and down like a rogue fairground ride.

At the front, Terry struggled happily with the controls.

"Fasten your seat belts, it's going to be a bumpy ride. Terry Small's airlines are about to whisk you away to exotic places," he said. He looked over at Ivan whose face was white with fear.

"Enjoying it, Boris? Want a sick bag?" he laughed, as the plane hurtled through the night.

"You fly too low," said Ivan.

"Yee-har! Ride 'em, cowboy!" said Terry, enjoying himself hugely. "We've got to keep low to stay underneath the radar, Boris," he explained. "Trust your Uncle Terry."

By now Ivan was too terrified to argue about names, altitude or anything. He took a tight grip on the arms of his seat and closed his eyes.

From the ground, Alison and Bill could only watch helplessly as the plane disappeared into the dark night sky.

"We must be able to do something. Can't we follow them in another plane?" said Alison desperately, rain pouring unnoticed down her face.

"Not in this storm. We'd never find them. But don't worry, when the radar picks them up, we can track them," said Bill.

"What about the storm? Will they be safe?" said Alison.

"I just hope that pilot is as good as he is crazy. Otherwise they could be in a lot of trouble," said Bill. They went back into the control tower, where the heavy rain battered the windows and the wind could be heard whistling round the airfield.

After some time, it became obvious that the plane was not going to show up on the tower's radar screens.

"They must be flying low enough to keep off the radar," said the Duty Controller. She and Bill knew just how dangerous that must be in the terrible storm. All they could do was watch as the weather got worse.

Bill spent several minutes on the phone.

When he returned he told Alison, "They've traced the van."

"And?"

"It was in London this afternoon. It's the same van that was used to kidnap an old man called Otto Scheer."

"Who's Otto Scheer?" said Alison, beginning to lose patience.

"During the Second World War, he was a gangster who specialised in looting church treasures from Eastern Europe," said Bill.

"Why was he kidnapped? Is he rich?"

"Just the opposite. Poor as the proverbial church mouse, apparently," explained Bill. "He was the only survivor of a plane crash at the end of the war. He lost his memory and a lot of the loot was never recovered."

"But it doesn't make sense. Why would they kidnap a poor old man?" said Alison, close to tears.

"I don't know, Allie. All the police could tell me was that the men are armed and very, very dangerous."

CHAPTER THREE

The storm continued for over an hour with the children imagining that every bump and dip could be their last. Finally, the plane left a huge cloud formation behind and burst out into clear sky. The roller-coaster ride was over.

For the first time the children had the chance to move around in their hiding place.

"Ouch. I've got cramp," announced Philip, stretching his legs.

"Keep it quiet. You'll get more than cramp if they hear you," whispered Dinah, pointing towards Terry chatting to Ivan at the front of the plane.

The children fell silent, trying to listen to the conversation.

"Father Paul, he in London still," said

Ivan, in his broken English.

"Well, we ain't going back for him now," said Terry. The change of plan meant that the meeting they'd arranged with the priest hadn't taken place. "He can come and meet us over there, can't he? Now, I'm going to have a word with our guest. Take over for a minute."

Terry got up from the pilot's seat, leaving a terrified Ivan at the controls.

"I no fly."

"It's easy. You just grab this and hold it steady," said Terry, casually. Ivan grabbed the wheel and the plane suddenly banked steeply.

"I said 'steady'," shouted Terry.

Ivan straightened the plane out of its dive. The children watched from their hiding place as Terry manhandled Otto out of his seat.

"I'm sorry about all this business, Fritz," said Terry, smiling insincerely.

"My name is Otto, not Fritz, you East End reject," said Otto angrily.

"Oh, you 'ave got the 'ump, ain't you, Fritz? There's no need for that. I just wanna

26

have a little chat..." Terry paused to keep Otto guessing.

"About what?"

"About that treasure you stashed away at the end of the war. The treasure you pretend you can't remember about."

Terry watched with satisfaction as Otto's eyes widened as he realised why he had been kidnapped.

"I cannot remember. My mind is a blank," he said quickly.

"Oh, is that right?" mocked Terry. "Well, my old dad's got a bad memory too. Shocking, it is. But he reckons a nice bit of fresh air helps him remember every time."

Terry hauled the old man towards the exit door of the plane and kicked it open. Wind howled through the plane's interior.

The powerful gusts of wind nearly lifted the sleeping bags off the children. They had to struggle to make sure they remained covered and unseen.

"Have a bit of fresh air, Fritz. Refresh your memory," said Terry cruelly, half-pushing Otto out of the aircraft door.

Ivan looked round from the controls to

see what was happening and the plane suddenly banked to one side.

Otto screamed in fear as he nearly fell out.

"Hey, don't do that, Boris. Old Fritz here nearly went sky-diving then," said Terry.

Only Terry's grip on Otto stopped him from falling. The wind threatened to pull the old man out of the aircraft at any second.

"Now, how's your memory doing?" asked Terry.

"I remember nothing," shouted Otto.

"I'll tell you what, mate. Nothing is exactly what you will remember if I let go of you. You've got five seconds..." threatened Terry.

"We've got to help him," whispered the terrified Dinah from her hiding place.

"Don't be mad," said Jack. "He'll only throw us all out!"

Terry's countdown began, "One... two... three..."

Otto looked at the ground far below. Suddenly the whole world seemed to spin. For a second his mind seemed to be back in the past. Back at the end of the Second World War. He saw the treasure and he knew where it was hidden.

"A valley! A valley in the Black Mountains!" It was as much of a revelation to him as it was to Terry. Perhaps his memory was coming back?

"Where exactly?" urged Terry.

"I cannot remember! I cannot remember even the name!" said Otto slowly. "There was no road, but there was a large lake and a river. I would recognise it from the air. We could only get into the valley by flying."

"Well, it's lucky we've got a plane then, innit?" said Terry, slamming the aircraft door shut and walking back to Ivan.

"The Black Mountains it is then," he said, taking over the controls and setting a new course.

The dawn sun filtered into the kitchen at Craggy Tops.

Alison was beside herself with worry about the children. Bill had been hoping that the plane would at last be spotted on radar by now, but no reports had come in from anywhere in the country.

"They've probably already landed somewhere," suggested Bill.

"Or crashed," said Alison dismally.

Bill moved closer to her. "There've been no reports of a crash or any wreckage being found," he said softly.

"So now what do we do?"

"If they're still in the air," said Bill, "we may get a visual contact. Trouble is, there's heavy cloud cover nearly everywhere."

Alison didn't like what she was hearing.

"So we do nothing? The children are flying God knows where with some madman and there's nothing we can do about it? What about your precious Department? Surely you can pull some strings?"

"They're going through all the intelligence files on anyone who could be involved in something like this. They'll find out who it is," said Bill, trying his best to reassure her.

"Even if we do find out who," said Alison close to tears, "we still won't know where they're going."

Flying several thousand feet above the Black Mountains in Germany, the children were dozing. Now that the storm was well behind them their flight was much calmer. They had taken it in turns to keep watch and so they had all been able to grab some sleep.

At the front of the plane, Terry was watching the ground with great interest. They were flying over beautiful mountains covered with green forests.

"Well, Fritz? There's the Black Mountains. Now, where's your little valley?" said Terry.

"I try to remember. We flew in many times."

"So there's a lot of treasure then, eh?" said Terry, with a big smile on his face.

"He say valley with no road," said Ivan, trying to help.

"That was over fifty years ago. For all we know there might be a flipping ski resort on top of his treasure trove by now," said Terry.

They began to fly over the area, covering

the valleys one by one. With each sweep Otto studied the ground beneath them carefully. Terry kept his eyes as much as he could on Otto's face, watching his reactions.

As they flew into yet another valley Terry saw Otto's eyes widen with surprise.

"You saw it, didn't you? You scheming old bird!" said Terry, with just a hint of admiration.

Terry circled the plane around and began his landing descent into the valley. The children could feel the plane heading down.

"We're landing at last," said Dinah. "What are we going to do?"

"Keep down and keep quiet until they get out," said Philip, thinking fast. "Then maybe we'll be able to get away."

The plane bumped along and came to a halt on a grassy field. There was a small derelict cottage over to one side. Its windows were all broken and it looked as if no one had been inside it for decades.

Terry opened the aircraft door and pushed Otto out.

"Looks deserted," said Terry, though he had his gun at the ready just in case.

"We killed them all, so no one could tell," said Otto. He looked as if was remembering things he'd hoped had gone away for good. "And we dynamited the only pass to stop anyone else getting in."

"You're a man after me own heart," said Terry, not at all shocked by this ghastly news. "We'll make base in that old cottage." He switched voices to one that sounded like a bored air hostess: "Thank you for flying Terry Small's Airlines. We hope you had a pleasant flight." And then back to normal again: "Come on, move it, Fritz!"

Ivan followed behind as Terry led Otto towards the ruins of the cottage. Philip watched from the plane window as the three men disappeared inside.

"All clear!" he said at last.

They crawled stiffly out from under the pile of sleeping bags and rucksacks that had kept them hidden for so long.

"I'm never going to play hide and seek again," announced Lucy-Ann indignantly.

"Good night! Good night!" said Kiki in her loudest squawk.

"You were clever, Kiki. Keeping quiet like that," said Dinah, patting her beak through the bars of the cage.

"Thank goodness it was night. She thought it was bedtime," smiled Jack.

"So what do we do now?" asked Lucy-Ann. "Otto said there were no roads round here and no people."

"We get out of here as fast as we can," said Philip firmly. "We can't hang around waiting for that maniac to find us. We're going to have to fend for ourselves."

CHAPTER FOUR

The children quickly gathered their things and opened the door to the plane. They climbed out awkwardly, carrying the sleeping bags, rucksacks and Kiki's cage. They knew they had to make their escape now, even though they risked being seen from the cottage – there was an even greater risk of being spotted if they stayed where they were.

"Quickly!" said Philip, hurrying the others along.

If Terry or Ivan had looked out of the broken windows of the cottage at that moment they would have seen the children leaving, but they were too busy tying Otto to an old wooden chair to notice anything else.

"Excuse," apologised Ivan as he

tightened the ropes.

Terry looked around at the derelict interior of the cottage. "Let's hope we don't have to stay here long. It's not exactly the Ritz."

"What is Ritz?" asked Ivan, his English not up to it.

"Forget it, Boris," said Terry, opening his mouth and letting out a terrific yawn. "I need to get some kip. Go and get them sleeping bags from the plane. I'll stay here and have a chat with old Fritzie boy about the treasure."

The four children trekked through the woods, with Philip leading the way. Behind him, Jack was carrying Kiki's cage. He didn't want to let her out in case she flew off and alerted the two men to their presence. But he was also worried about what they were going to do next.

"Philip, where are we heading?" he asked.

"As far away from those thugs as possible," said Philip simply.

"Well, can we stop and make a proper

plan?" said Jack.

Philip stopped and turned round. "OK, Einstein. What's the plan then?" he said sarcastically.

"We're all tired and hungry. Before we do anything else I think we should find a safe place to eat and get some sleep," suggested Jack.

"Jack's right," said Dinah. "And there's no hurry, those men don't even know we're here."

Lucy-Ann had been scouting ahead and had caught sight of something in the distance. "Hey, there's an old barn over here," she called to the others.

The children picked up their gear and wove through the trees towards the barn.

"All right," said Philip. "We'll rest in here, but we've got to take turns to keep watch." He led the way into the dim interior of the barn. It was full of piles of wood and junk, and a row of rusting old farm machinery lined one wall.

"Let's find somewhere to sleep," said Lucy-Ann, looking round.

Jack put Kiki's cage down and opened it

so the bird could fly out and stretch her wings. Kiki stepped bravely out. "Clever Kiki! Clever Kiki!" she said.

"What an amazing place this is!" said Lucy-Ann, who kept finding old and exciting things in the barn. She grabbed a handful of straw and sent it spiralling into the air. "Wheee!"

Dinah walked straight into a spider's web. "Yuck!" she said. She loathed creepy-crawlies of any sort, and the sticky webbing was all over her hair.

Jack watched Kiki fly up to the barn roof past the loft ladder. "Me and Kiki will keep first watch," he said, climbing up. "Not that there'll be much to watch," he smiled.

At Craggy Tops, Bill was on the phone once again. Alison waited anxiously by his side for news.

"That sounds like our man. Now, find him! And find him fast," said Bill, ending the conversation.

"What's happening?" said Alison, before Bill could even replace the receiver.

"A few days ago, Father Paul, an old

Russian priest, came to England. His church was one of those ransacked by Otto Scheer at the end of the war. My Department has just found out that apparently Father Paul has made it his life's work to track down Otto Scheer," explained Bill.

"You think the priest found Otto Scheer and then had him kidnapped? So if we can find the priest...?" said Alison, thinking aloud.

"He may lead us to Otto... and..."

"And the children!" finished Alison with a smile. Bill nodded.

Ivan ran back towards the cottage as fast as he could. He could hardly contain himself.

"Is gone!" he shouted, bursting inside.

"What's gone?" said Terry.

"I go to plane like you say. Only no sleeping bags. They gone. Vanish," said Ivan, shrugging his shoulders.

"Gone? How could they have gone? Otto, I thought you said there was no one left here?" said Terry, turning to the helpless Otto.

"That is right."

"And there's no way into the valley?" asked Terry.

"No. None at all. We chose it well," said Otto, with a touch of pride.

"Then either we've got ghosts or someone else was on that plane," announced Terry.

"There is no one left in the valley. They all died," said Otto.

"Yeah, well, whoever took them bags is gonna die as well. We don't want no sightseers." Terry took out his gun and checked its bullets. "Come on, Boris. Let's get 'em."

Terry lead Ivan out of the cottage. They stopped at the plane to grab a pair of binoculars, then they headed into the woods.

The hunt was on.

CHAPTER FIVE

Terry and Ivan had been searching for over an hour. Terry had scanned most of the valley with his binoculars but had seen no signs of life.

This time, however, was different.

He had looked at the old barn before, but on this sweep, Terry caught sight of Jack sitting in the high roof window.

A broad grin spread across Terry's face.

"Come on, Boris," he said.

Terry and Ivan tried to make as little noise as possible as they approached the building. However, as neither of them was used to walking through thick woods there was a lot of twig snapping and cursing from the men as they walked unexpectedly into a small stream.

Jack, still keeping the first watch, heard

them heading towards him. He raced down from the loft to alert the others.

"They're coming! They're coming! Quick! Out the back door!" he said, making sure everyone picked up all their belongings. If they left anything behind, it would be obvious to the two men that someone had been here.

The four children rushed outside.

"Which way?" asked Philip.

"Over here," said Jack. He led them round the side of the barn, but then saw that Terry and Ivan had chosen to try and sneak through the trees the same way.

"Back! Back!" he called, as quietly as he could, leading them back the other way. They took cover in a bushy hollow where they wouldn't be seen.

"Jack!" cried Dinah, who was behind him. "Your rucksack! You've left it behind!" In the commotion, Jack had forgotten his own bag.

"Leave it!" yelled Lucy-Ann as Jack turned round to hurry back to the barn.

"No! If they find it, they'll know somebody's been here for sure," said Jack, who didn't know that they'd already been spotted.

He ran back to the barn with Dinah following him, and raced up the ladder to where he'd left his rucksack. Kiki flew towards him, expecting a friendly shoulder to land on, but Jack didn't have time.

From their position in the hollow, Philip and Lucy-Ann watched in horror as Terry and Ivan came closer to the barn.

Terry pulled out his gun.

Jack was trapped inside the loft as Terry and Ivan silently opened the front door and crept inside. The two men peered through the shadows towards the piles of junk and old farm machines.

Then there was the sound of a loud police siren just above their heads. Terry and Ivan panicked and ran outside.

"Kiki!" whispered Lucy-Ann from the safety of the hollow. "That was her police siren impression!"

Terry and Ivan had stopped outside the barn and were now feeling more than a little foolish.

"Someone's playing tricks, Boris," said

Terry, leading them back inside.

Jack opened the window in the loft, and began to climb out on to the roof, his feet struggling to find a safe grip on the cracked slates. If only he could hide till the men had gone! He could hear them resuming their search on the ground floor.

"Wipe your feet! Shut the door!" screamed Kiki suddenly.

Terry spun round and fired his gun at the noise. He caught a fleeting glimpse of Kiki as she flew towards Jack on the roof and let off several more bullets.

Outside, the children jumped as they heard the loud shots echo through the valley. Where was Jack?

"Stop that noise! Be quiet!" said Kiki loudly from one of the rafters. Terry and Ivan exchanged a puzzled look. They didn't know what to think!

Outside, on the roof, Jack was perched in a dangerous position. He only had one good hand-hold and was having difficulty moving around. He stretched forward gingerly, but his hand slipped and the movement dislodged a slate.

"Oh no!" he cried silently to himself.

The slate clattered loudly to the ground, the noise bringing Terry and Ivan out of the barn. They looked around for a moment, then glanced down to the ground and saw the fallen slate in pieces on the ground. Terry looked up to the roof but there was no sign of anyone.

He took a couple of steps back and looked again. Now he could see something! Jack's fingers were holding on to the apex of the roof from the other side. He thought a moment, then decided to try a trick.

"There's no one here," he said loudly, gesturing to Ivan. "They must have gone. Let's get back."

Ivan looked puzzled, but followed Terry away from the barn.

"But he's up on the roof," Ivan whispered, confused.

"I know," whispered Terry back, "but I don't want him to know that we know."

Now Ivan was even more confused, but he followed behind as Terry signalled for him to head round the side of the building.

Philip, Dinah, and Lucy-Ann watched the action from the safety of their hollow. They were desperate to warn Jack, but Terry and Ivan were between them and the barn and there was no way they could do so.

They saw Jack slowly making his way back over the ridge of the roof as quietly as he could. He looked down and, as he could see no sign of Terry or Ivan below him, he inched quietly towards the loft window he'd climbed out of earlier. As he got nearer he heard a familiar parrot noise coming from just inside the window.

"Kiki?" he whispered.

Jack leant forward and opened the wooden shutters of the window – and found himself looking straight into the barrel of Terry's gun.

"Who's a pretty boy, then?" smiled Terry.

CHAPTER SIX

"They've caught Jack!" said Dinah, ducking further under cover in case the men should come out and look for the others.

The three children watched as Terry and Ivan suddenly appeared from inside the barn. Jack was walking in front of them at gunpoint.

"We've got to save him," said Lucy-Ann, desperate to help her brother.

"We will, but we can't rush them now," said Philip calmly. "We'll follow them and see where they take Jack."

They raced through the trees, making sure that they kept Terry and the others in sight at all times. They ended up back to the ramshackle cottage where Otto was still tied up.

"Did you miss us, Fritz?" asked Terry as they walked in. "Never mind, we've brought some company for you." He sat Jack down, produced a length of rope and began to tie him to the chair.

Outside, the three children carefully moved towards the cottage until they could see in through the window. Before they could decide what to do, a huge thunderclap exploded above them, its sound echoing along the sides of the valley. It looked as though the heavens were about to open!

"We need to find somewhere safe to hide, out of the rain," said Dinah.

"But what about Jack?" asked Lucy-Ann, watching helplessly as her brother was tied up.

"We'll leave a trail so we can find our way back, then we'll come back and try a rescue later," said Dinah.

"I don't want to leave Jack," said Lucy-Ann firmly.

"We've got to, Lucy-Ann. We can't help him now," said Philip, leading the others away.

The children scrambled through a rocky area that led up the side of the valley. Philip stopped every hundred feet or so and tied a piece of string on to a tree branch so they could retrace their route. Suddenly a flash of lightning illuminated the whole valley, followed by another deafening crack of thunder. Heavy drops of rain began to hit the ground.

"We're going to get soaked," wailed Lucy-Ann.

A parrot squawk sounded ahead of them somewhere in the trees.

"It's Kiki! Where is she?" said Philip, looking for her.

"It came from over there," said Dinah, pointing towards a small opening in the rockface. The children ran over to it and found Kiki perched on a large rock.

"It's a cave! Kiki's found us a cave!" said Dinah, examining the entrance.

"More like a mouse hole from the looks of it," sighed Philip, peering into it.

"Well, at least it's something," said Lucy-Ann, pushing past Philip and climbing inside.

"Lucy-Ann, wait!" said Dinah, surprised at her unexpected boldness.

Lucy-Ann plunged deeper into the cave. "Come on! It's bigger than you think," she called.

The others followed her inside, grimacing at the small size. It was really more of a thin fissure in the rocks than a proper cave.

"We'll have to take turns to sit down," said Philip.

"At least it's out of the rain," said Dinah, hearing the downpour that was beginning outside.

"Turn on the light! Turn on the light!" said Kiki, sitting on a ledge above them. She didn't like the dark.

Philip was checking to see whether there was anywhere else they could sit. He saw that behind where Kiki was perched there seemed to be another passage.

"I wonder what's through there?" he said, clambering on to the ledge and peering through. "Looks like there might be more room, but not a lot."

"More room! More room! Mind the

doors!" squawked Kiki.

Rain began to trickle down the sides of the fissure, dislodging small bits of rock. The three children looked back towards the entrance as another flash of lightning lit up the valley.

"The storm's getting worse," said Lucy-Ann, trying hard not to sound scared.

Jack's arms, tied behind his back, were beginning to hurt. He was being interrogated by Terry and was inventing some excellent lies.

"I stowed away on the plane," he repeated for the third time.

"What for?" asked Terry.

"I've run away from home," lied Jack.

Terry moved closer and leant down so he was staring straight into Jack's eyes. "Who else was with you?"

"No one. I'm on my own. Where are we? I want to go home."

"Well, now, my son," Terry mocked. "You should have thought about that before you got on the plane."

Jack could see he wasn't getting anywhere.

"I won't tell anybody anything, I promise," he appealed.

"Oh, you won't tell anybody, all right," said Terry, with a cruel grin. "I'll see to that."

Torrential rain beat against the entrance to the cave. The storm raged around them and all the children could do was wait it out.

"If it keeps on like this, it'll wash the whole cave away," said Dinah.

The biggest lightning flash yet exploded and Lucy-Ann let out a piercing scream. There was a strange cracking sound above them as if a rock was being cleft in two.

"What was that?" said Philip in a worried voice.

Kiki let out a loud squawk and flew deeper into the cave. There was another thunderous roar, but for once it wasn't the weather. Pieces of rock began to fall down on the three children.

"We're going to be buried!" screamed Dinah.

Philip pushed the girls deeper into the

cavern. "Through here," he gasped.

Behind them, a large boulder crashed down near the hole they had used to get inside. Lucy-Ann screamed as the boulder's impact sent rock fragments flying through the air.

"It's gone totally dark," she said, reaching into her rucksack for her torch. She found it and shone a beam of light back towards the entrance.

It was completely blocked by fallen rock.

"We're trapped," said Dinah softly. "Buried underground."

CHAPTER SEVEN

Terry and Ivan stood huddled together in conversation in the ruined cottage.

"We bring Father Paul now," said Ivan.

"What for?" asked Terry. "We haven't found the treasure yet."

"Father Paul want to be here," insisted Ivan.

"Later, Boris."

"My name Ivan."

As usual Terry ignored him. "Later. After old Fritzie tells us where the treasure is. And you are gonna tell us, ain't you, Fritzie baby?" said Terry, sitting down to face Otto.

"I - I can't remember clearly," said Otto, looking across to Jack for support.

"Oh, I'm sure you can if you try," said Terry.

Jack's head spun round in alarm as Terry cocked his gun.

"Now you've got your memory back, I'm sure it's as clear as the bullets up this spout, ain't it, Fritzie?" said Terry, aiming the gun at Otto.

"If you shoot him, you'll never find what you're looking for," interrupted Jack cockily.

"Button it!" snapped Terry. He moved closer to Otto.

"We'll find the treasure with or without you, Fritzie. It may take a little longer with you six feet under the ground, but we'll find it now that we're here."

Otto looked Terry in the eye. "What would you do with it if you found it? It's not yours."

"It wasn't yours either, was it?" smiled Terry. "You stole it. You were a very naughty boy."

Ivan stepped forward, his eyes staring accusingly at Otto. "Father Paul want the Golden Madonna. He take it back home to his church. To his people."

Jack listened carefully, gradually piecing

the story together.

"And what about the rest of the treasure? I suppose you'll keep that for yourselves?" needled Otto.

"Reward," said Ivan.

"There's a big reward for taking that stuff back where it belongs," grinned Terry. "It'd make a lot of people very happy."

A look of innocence suddenly appeared on Otto's face. "Maybe, maybe I share the reward with you?"

"You?" said Terry incredulously. He could hardly believe his ears.

"If I show you where the treasure is hidden?" Otto went on.

Terry was not exactly an expert on moral dilemmas at the best of times, but this idea had him really stumped.

"Well, I don't know, Fritz, to be honest. You've got me there. I mean, you stole the treasure in the first place, didn't you?" said Terry.

"But the war was over long ago. Now, I have nothing. I get some reward too, maybe?" said Otto keenly.

Terry saw how he could work the

situation to his own advantage. Otto was much more likely to reveal where the treasure was if there was something in it for him.

"Yeah, I think you're right. I'm sure they'd give you something. They're bound to," encouraged Terry.

Otto smiled. "I am too weak to go, but I make a map."

Terry smiled. "Make it a good one, then."

Ivan untied Otto and then looked for a piece of charcoal from the fireplace. Terry picked up Jack's rucksack and rummaged through the contents until he pulled out a white T-shirt.

"There isn't any paper, but this'll do," he said, throwing it to Otto.

"Hey, that's mine!" cried Jack, struggling against his bonds.

"Don't worry, midget," said Terry unkindly. "You ain't going to need it again."

Otto got working on the map. Using the charcoal to draw on the T-shirt was difficult, but Otto went as fast as he could.

Terry and Ivan stood by his side watching every new line intently.

"That looks like a cave," said Terry, half talking to himself. "And that's were we are now."

"Where? There?" whispered Ivan, pointing.

"Don't be daft," jeered Terry. "That's not the plane. That's a tree."

The charcoal slipped out of Otto's fingers and fell to the floor. He leant down and picked it up while Terry and Ivan studied the emerging map, then paused for just a second before slipping a small piece of slate into his other hand.

As he did this, Otto's eyes met Jack's across the other side of the room. Jack smiled at Otto, but as Otto's expression did not change, he looked away in disappointment. Maybe whatever Otto was planning did not involve Jack. Otto straightened up and slipped the slate into his jacket pocket.

"Come on, get on with it," ordered Terry.

Otto returned to his work. "Almost

finished, my friends, almost finished," he promised.

Philip crawled along the tunnel, holding his torch in front of him. Now there was no way out behind them, their only chance lay in following this tunnel. Surely it must lead somewhere?

"Can you see what's ahead?" called Dinah from behind.

Philip shone the torch forwards, but the yellow beam only lit up more tunnel. There was still no sign of daylight.

"Nothing yet," said Philip, trying not to sound too disappointed.

"We must have come miles," said Lucy-Ann. She was getting very tired, and it was difficult to crawl with a heavy rucksack on.

"At least it's wide enough for us to keep going," said Philip.

"But what if it doesn't lead anywhere? What if it's just a dead end? The tunnel is so small there isn't enough room for us to turn round and go back," said Dinah.

"There wouldn't be any point in going back, would there?" said Philip bluntly.

"We know very well that we can't get out at that end. We've got to keep going."

The three children crawled on along the cold and twisting tunnel. Each move took more effort than the last.

After another twenty minutes Lucy-Ann had had enough. "I've got to stop. I can't carry on," she said, exhausted.

"You've got to. We can't give up," said Philip. Then he thought about what would motivate Lucy-Ann the most. "Jack is relying on us to rescue him."

"Let's rest for a while. Whatever is at the end will still be there in a few minutes," said Dinah, acting as peacemaker. She was tired too.

The children lay panting on the floor of the tunnel. Philip turned off his torch. They could see nothing in the pitch black.

"What did you do that for?" said Dinah.

"Saving the batteries. We don't know how much further we have to go," answered Philip.

They lay in silence, their eyes adjusting to the new darkness.

Lucy-Ann flicked her finger against the

side of her own torch then propped herself up on one elbow. Something had caught her attention.

"What's that?

"What?" said Philip impatiently.

"That noise."

"I don't hear any..."

"Sshh!" insisted Lucy-Ann.

The three children listened in the total dark of the tunnel. They strained their ears for any slight sound. Out of the blackness, far away, came a faint but eerie roar.

It was water. Fast flowing water.

"That could be good news," said Philip, "or it could mean that the tunnel is flooding. We've got to find a way out."

The children scrambled on as fast as they could move.

CHAPTER EIGHT

The three children crawled round a corner in the tunnel.

"Look, it's starting to widen out!" said Philip with relief.

Lucy-Ann was hopeful. "It's got to be the way out of here," she said.

Ahead of them the tunnel took another sharp turn to the right.

"Stay here," said Philip, "I'll scout ahead."

Philip cautiously approached the second bend. As he went nearer to where the rock curved round, the sound of flowing water became much louder. He stepped round the corner and pointed his torch ahead of him. He was delighted by what he saw.

"Come here! It's OK! Come on!" he

called back to the others.

The girls, hearing the excitement in his voice, joined him as fast as they could. Ahead of them, the tunnel opened out into a waterfall and beyond that, daylight.

"We're behind a waterfall!" cried Lucy-Ann.

"All fall down! All fall down!" cried Kiki as she flew over Lucy-Ann's shoulder.

They were standing on a flat platform behind the rushing curtain of the waterfall itself, which splashed down into a blue lagoon that stretched out before the children.

"This is amazing," said Lucy-Ann.

"It's perfect. No one could ever find us here," added Dinah.

"What do you think, Kiki?" said Lucy-Ann.

"Clever Kiki! Clever Kiki!" said the parrot. Lucy-Ann picked her up.

Hanging by the side of the waterfall were thick green creepers. Philip gave one a tug, but it came away in his hand.

"These creepers won't be strong enough for us to climb down to ground level," he said. "I'll fix up a rcpe so we can use that."

"And while you're doing that..." said Dinah, pulling a huge bar of chocolate from her rucksack, "we'll have breakfast."

Lucy-Ann smiled and gave Kiki a stroke. "And after that," she said, her tiredness forgotten,"we'll go and rescue Jack."

Father Paul was waiting calmly at the police station for the arrival of Bill. He'd been tracked to his hotel by Bill's Department. Policemen had "invited" the Russian priest to accompany them to the police station for an interview.

Bill finally entered the room and shook hands with Father Paul.

"I can't imagine what this is about, Mr..?" said Father Paul.

"Cunningham, Bill Cunningham," Bill said.

"Mr Cunningham. But of course, I'll help in anyway I can," said Father Paul.

Bill switched on the big tape machine on the table between them.

"Thank you, Father Paul. First, then,

would you mind telling us why you came to London?" said Bill.

"Not at all. I came here to visit my nephew, Ivan," said Father Paul. "But sadly he has left town and no one can tell me where he has gone. Now I must return home without seeing him."

"So you didn't come here to see Otto Scheer?" said Bill, watching Father Paul's reaction very carefully.

"Otto Scheer?" said Father Paul blankly. "I thought he was dead, long ago."

"Otto Scheer was kidnapped on a London street yesterday. He was abducted and taken by plane to an unknown destination," said Bill, still watching Father Paul's face.

So far he had the impression that none of this was news to the Russian priest.

"Unfortunately, there were four children on the plane as well, and they were kidnapped too," went on Bill, this time seeing the expression of surprise on Father Paul's face. His own face hardened. "Now, I don't really care what happens to Scheer, but I don't want those children harmed."

"Of course not, of course not," said Father Paul, hiding his emotions once more. "It all sounds very unfortunate."

"The description of one of the kidnappers sounds a lot like your nephew," said Bill, passing the photofit picture across the table.

Father Paul merely glanced at it. "There must be some mistake," he said. "Ivan is a – how shall I say it? – a simple boy." Father Paul tapped the side of his head significantly. "He wouldn't think of doing such a thing," he continued, handing the picture back.

"But maybe he's helping someone more clever," Bill suggested. "Someone who could plan such a thing? His uncle for example?"

Father Paul let out a relaxed laugh. "Me? Mr Cunningham, you make me out to be much smarter than I am. What would a humble priest know about kidnapping?"

"Don't play games with me, Father." Bill's voice was curt. "If Otto Scheer knows where your Golden Madonna is hidden then we can help you get it back." He leant forward and looked the priest straight in the eyes. "Now please, if you know where they've taken Scheer and the children, tell me."

Father Paul paused for a moment as if weighing up his options.

"I'm sorry, Mr Cunningham, I haven't any idea where they can be. You are wrong in thinking that I am involved."

Bill reached forward and turned off the tape recorder. He could see he was wasting his time.

Otto had finished drawing his map.

Ivan held the T-shirt with it on, while Terry tied Otto to his chair again. He was now sitting directly behind Jack with his back to him.

"It's not that we don't trust you, Fritz, but we don't want you wandering about the woods on your own now, do we? You might get lost and miss out on your reward," said Terry.

Terry tied the ropes so tight that they hurt Otto's arm.

"Is too tight," moaned Otto.

"Get used to it," barked Terry. He looked over to Ivan. "All right, let's go treasure hunting."

Terry and Ivan left the cottage and headed away into the woods. Otto watched them through a broken window until they were out of sight.

"Now what?" said Jack. He tested his ropes, but they were quite firm.

Behind him, Jack could hear Otto straining against his bonds. Otto reached into his pocket and pulled out the piece of slate that he had hidden earlier.

"Here, boy, take this and cut my ropes," said Otto, passing the slate to Jack's hand. Otto could not reach his own ropes but, sitting behind him, Jack could.

"I thought you were planning something like this," said Jack, taking the piece of slate. He carefully began to work on the ropes that held Otto with the sharp side.

"Hurry!" said Otto anxiously. "*Schnell! Schnell!*"

"What's the rush?" questioned Jack. "They'll be ages finding the treasure and digging it up."

"They won't be away that long," said Otto. "Not when they work out that the map is false."

Jack's eyes widened in alarm as he realised that the pair could return at any time. He pushed the slate against the ropes and redoubled his efforts.

CHAPTER NINE

"This is nothing like it!" said Terry, stopping by the bank of a fast-flowing river. He looked down at the map and tried to match it with the terrain around them, but nothing seemed to make sense. For a start, there was no river on the map.

"It's a joke!" said Terry in disgust.

Ivan took the map from Terry and looked for himself. "Is not funny," he commented.

"That stupid old fool has tried to pull a fast one on us. Let's get back to the cottage and sort him out," said Terry, bunching up the T-shirt and throwing it into the river.

"But Father Paul must have the Golden Madonna," said Ivan. "How we make Otto tell truth?"

"Don't worry. When we get back, it's no

70

more Mr Nice Guy from me," said Terry.

The object of their anger was close to escape. Jack had been working hard on Otto's ropes.

"Nearly there," said Jack, trying hard to see behind him. "Hang on..."

The ropes frayed and then gave way. Otto lifted his hands up and rubbed his wrists. He was free!

"Ah! Good work, boy," said Otto, leaning down to untie the rest of his bonds. "Now, let's get out of here before they come back." He moved over to Jack and started to undo the ropes that held him.

"How long do you think it will take them to work out the map is wrong?" asked Jack.

"Not long. I just made it up. Probably nothing on it is like what's round here."

Otto's old fingers struggled with the tight knots that Terry had tied, but in a few minutes Jack was free.

"Come on!" said Jack, grabbing his rucksack.

"We go for the treasure now," said Otto

with a nod.

"No, let's find my friends first," said Jack.

"Friends?" Otto was surprised.

"You're not the only one who can fool people," smiled Jack.

Suddenly they both stopped dead.

"Did you hear that, boy?" murmured Otto.

"Yeah, someone's coming through the woods behind the cottage. Let's go!" cried Jack, pushing Otto ahead of him out of the door. They headed off down the valley in the direction of the old barn.

The rustling near the back of the cottage got louder. Three faces poked out of the undergrowth looking towards the crumbling building. It was Philip, Dinah and Lucy-Ann.

"Wait! There's someone over there," said Philip, ducking back down.

The figures they had caught sight of were, of course, Jack and Otto leaving, but the children could not see them clearly enough to know who they were.

They waited for a few minutes,

72

watching from the safety of the undergrowth.

"I can't see anyone inside the cottage," said Lucy-Ann.

"Maybe they've gone?" said Dinah.

Philip carefully stepped forward, keeping as quiet as he could. "I'll go and see."

"Be careful, Philip," said Dinah.

"I wasn't exactly planning to go and knock on the door," whispered Philip.

He began to creep towards the side of the cottage, keeping out of sight of the windows. He bent down under the nearest one and cautiously took a peek inside.

The cottage was empty.

Philip walked round to the front and went inside to search the place.

"There's no one there. They must have moved on," said Lucy-Ann, watching from the undergrowth. She stood up and headed off to join Philip.

Suddenly Dinah grabbed her and pulled her down. "Wait! Look over there! Someone's coming!"

The girls ran round the side of the

cottage. From there they could see Terry and Ivan making their way along the edge of the woods.

"It's the kidnappers! We've got to warn Philip," said Lucy-Ann. She turned and ran towards the cottage.

Inside, Philip was kneeling down, examining the ropes that Jack had cut during his escape.

"They're coming!" cried Lucy-Ann as she dashed towards him.

"We've got to find somewhere to hide," said Philip, looking around.

Terry and Ivan had reached the door of the cottage.

"Now we're gonna get the truth out of that old coot," said Terry as they came inside.

Philip and Lucy-Ann slipped into the shadows, pressing themselves against the wall. "They're bound to see us," whispered Lucy-Ann.

As they entered, however, Terry's attention was fixed firmly on the empty chairs.

"They've escaped!" he said angrily.

"How?" said Ivan.

"Who cares?" Terry was furious. He picked up one of the chairs and threw it across the room. It smashed against the wall opposite.

Ivan followed Terry outside again.

"We'll find them. The old man can't have got very far," said Terry, starting to scan the woods through his binoculars.

He smiled as he focused on two figures heading down the valley. "Got them! They're heading for that barn. Come on."

Terry and Ivan gave chase.

Dinah joined Philip and Lucy-Ann inside the cottage. Through a window they watched Terry and Ivan run into the distance.

"We've got to warn Jack that they're coming after him," said Philip.

"But how?" said Dinah. "We can't get there first."

"If only we hadn't left the distress flares back at the waterfall," said Lucy-Ann, thinking aloud.

"Signalling is the right idea," said

Philip. "But what with?" Philip looked round. In the corner of the room was a pile of tatty old rags. Philip picked two of them up.

"What are you going to do with those?" asked Lucy-Ann.

"Just watch," said Philip, leading the way outside.

Jack and Otto made their way down the valley towards the barn.

"We go for the treasure now," said Otto, looking back over his shoulder.

"No. I want to find my friends first. When we find them they can help us," said Jack. He'd had this discussion before and he was getting tired of it.

"We left a gun behind with the treasure. It will still be there. We need it to protect ourselves from the English mad-dog," said Otto, trying a new argument.

"It'll be really old now. It probably wouldn't work anyway after all this time," said Jack, climbing over a fallen tree trunk.

Otto thought back to the old days. "It might work. It was a good weapon," he said.

"Well, I'm still going to look for my friends," said Jack firmly. He plotted his own course through the trees ahead and set off.

Otto watched him go with a slightly exasperated look on his face.

"You know what you want to do, boy. I give you that," he said, following behind.

Jack headed up a steep incline, pulling himself higher by using trees as handholds. Near the top he paused to help Otto climb the last few metres.

"Your friends could be anywhere. We should go on," said Otto, getting his breath back.

Jack took his binoculars out of his rucksack and began scanning the valley. They had a good view right back to where the plane had landed.

Jack focused in on the cottage. Yes! There was Philip and the girls.

Philip was holding the two rags in his outstretched hands and using them as makeshift semaphore flags.

"It's Philip!" said Jack to Otto. "I knew

we'd find him. He's sending a message.

Jack watched as Philip used the flags to spell out the message one letter at a time.

" - G - , - E -, - R -," read Jack. "Ger?"

Otto grabbed the binoculars from Jack and watched Philip signal the next letters. " - D - , - A - , - N - ."

"Ger Dan?" said Otto, puzzled.

"Dan-ger. Danger!" said Jack. "That's what he's saying. We're in danger!"

CHAPTER TEN

Alison paced anxiously round the kitchen at Craggy Tops. There had been no further news. Talking to Father Paul had been a waste of time, and Bill's stolen plane had still not been sighted.

Bill watched Alison, knowing how upset she was.

"Try not to worry," he said. "My Department are watching the priest day and night. We're all sure he's behind Otto's kidnapping, and when he makes his move, we'll follow him." Bill hoped this would reassure her.

"You really think he's in on it?" said Alison.

"I think he'll lead us straight to Otto... and the children."

"But if Father Paul knows where this

man Otto Scheer is, why doesn't he go to the police and ask for their help?" asked Alison.

"He's been after Otto Scheer for over half a century. It's too personal for him to let the authorities take over," explained Bill. "It's not just his Golden Madonna he wants. It's revenge."

Jack scanned the valley with his binoculars from the higher ground of the woods. He and Otto had moved there after Philip had warned them that they were being followed. He looked back to the old barn and focused on the two figures approaching it. They were Terry, with gun in hand, and Ivan.

"They're just going into the barn," said Jack to Otto.

"Never mind, boy. We keep moving, yes? They don't know where we are now," said Otto.

Jack slipped his binoculars back into his rucksack and followed behind him.

As Jack and Otto moved away they lost sight of the building behind a ridge of tall pine trees. They did not see Terry and Ivan come outside after a few minutes and search the area round the barn.

"There's loads of footprints in that hollow over there. Recent ones. I reckon we've got more uninvited guests than I thought," said Terry, annoyed. "And I bet our tricky little friend is leading them straight to the treasure."

Ivan walked away from the barn and knelt down to examine the ground.

"They could be flipping anywhere," said Terry, getting angrier by the minute, but Ivan, the methodical one, had found something interesting.

"That way," he said, pointing up into the rising woodland in front of them. Terry came over and looked at what Ivan had found.

Jack and Otto had passed by the barn earlier. Jack's training shoe had left a muddy footprint as he walked over a rock – a footprint which was still wet. It was the perfect pointer to where Jack and Otto were heading.

"You're not just a pretty face, are you,

Boris?" smiled Terry, cheering up again. They headed off through the trees at a running pace.

Half an hour later, Otto and Jack were still walking through the thick woods.

"Not far to go. We stop and get our breath back," said Otto, panting a little.

"So you really do remember where you hid the treasure?" asked Jack. He hadn't believed in Otto's convenient loss of memory.

"For years I could remember nothing," Otto protested. "But just now, in the plane, suddenly it all came rushing back. I remember like it was yesterday and..."

"Sshh!" said Jack, who had suddenly heard movement in the trees nearby. "Quick! Hide!"

They ducked down into the undergrowth and disappeared from view just as Philip, Dinah and Lucy-Ann came rushing through the trees.

"Lucy-Ann!" called Jack as soon as he saw his sister. Lucy-Ann ran straight over to him and gave him a big hug, which rather embarrassed him.

"You're safe!" she exclaimed.

"'Course I am, ninny," said Jack, blushing.

"Did you see our signal?" asked Philip. "They were coming after you."

"I think we lost them down near the barn. Thanks for the warning," smiled Jack.

"We've found this brilliant cave with a waterfall where they'll never find us," said Lucy-Ann.

Otto suddenly let out a painful groan and sat down on the ground.

"Are you all right?" said Jack, leaning down to help him.

"I need rest," said Otto wearily.

"You'd better take us to this cave of yours, then," said Jack to Lucy-Ann. "Then Otto can rest there."

"We left a trail of string on the branches of the trees so we could find it again," said Dinah. "I'll lead the way."

With Philip's help, Jack got Otto to his feet and the five of them set off. At first they made good progress, but then the terrain became rocky and the walking more difficult. Otto was exhausted and could hardly go on. The boys did their very best to support him, but it was hard work.

"I – can't – go – so fast," said Otto, completely out of breath. "You must go on and get the gun."

"Gun? What gun?" said Philip. It was the first he'd heard of it.

"There's a gun hidden with the treasure," explained Jack. "Otto thinks it'll still work."

"What, after all these years?" said Philip doubtfully.

"Yes! It good gun. Very good gun!" insisted Otto, who was getting fed up with people saying that it wouldn't work. Now he was anxious to reach a safe place where he could rest – but he would be happier still if someone could bring him the gun as well.

"You must follow the curve of the river until you find a small hill," he said to the two boys. "The cave entrance is marked by a rock that has the shape of a bear. You must bring the gun back to me."

"I think we should get you to a safe hiding place first," said Jack.

At that moment there was a movement in the bushes behind them. The children and Otto spun round just as Terry stepped out, gun in hand.

"Got you!" he said, grinning from ear to ear.

CHAPTER ELEVEN

Lucy-Ann opened her mouth wide and let out her loudest scream.

"Run for it!" shouted Jack as Terry advanced towards the group, and before Terry could stop them, the four children raced into the trees.

"Hold it!" shouted Terry. He raised his gun to fire, but Ivan knocked down his arm. The children disappeared out of sight.

"They are only children," said Ivan in his thick Russian accent. "I will find them."

Ivan hurried off into the woods, leaving Otto alone with Terry. Otto jumped to his feet as Terry grabbed hold of his lapels.

"You told them where the treasure is, didn't you, Fritz?" said Terry angrily.

The children kept running until they were

sure that Terry was not following them. It took them only about ten minutes to make their way to the river gorge.

"Safe at last," said Philip, giving Jack a smile. "What do you think?"

Jack looked round, trying to take everything in.

The beautiful waterfall cascaded down into the lagoon. With the light from the sunset outside filtering into the gorge it looked amazing.

"Unreal!"

The four children and Kiki made their way along the ledge that led to the waterfall and the hidden cave beyond it. Lucy-Ann had fallen behind the others and Philip waited for her to catch up. "Come on," he urged.

"I'm tired out," complained Lucy-Ann, sinking exhausted to the ground.

Philip took hold of the rope that was the only way up to the cave itself. He helped Jack start his climb, then gave Dinah a hand.

"Come on, Lucy-Ann," said Philip, beginning his own climb up.

"I still haven't got my breath back," said Lucy-Ann.

"I'm not leaving you down there. You can do it."

Lucy-Ann didn't move.

"You've got to!" shouted Jack.

"Slave-driver!" said Lucy-Ann. She picked herself up slowly, grinning. She took the rope in her hands and, summoning the last of her will-power, started to climb towards the upper ledge.

She got halfway to the top when her arms just seemed to give up.

"Come on! Grab my hand!" called Jack, reaching down as far as he could.

"I can't! I can't!" said Lucy-Ann. She really was exhausted. She struggled up, but Jack's hand was out of her reach. Her fingers touched Jack's for just a second, then she lost her grip on the rope and fell.

She plummeted towards the lagoon directly below her.

Lucy-Ann let out an ear-piercing scream that echoed round the gorge. Then her cry was silenced by the blue water as she plunged beneath the surface.

Lucy-Ann's scream even reached outside the gorge to Ivan, who had been doing his best to track the children. He'd followed their own trail of pieces of string tied on to the branches of trees, but he'd lost the trail close to the entrance to the gorge. Then, luckily for him, he heard Lucy-Ann's echoing scream and headed towards the source of the sound.

Inside the gorge, Philip had come down to pull Lucy-Ann out of the water. She was quite unharmed, but very cold and very wet.

"If you so much as smile you'll be in here too," she threatened, as Philip pulled her out.

"Would I ever laugh at such a tragic incident?" said Philip, unable to keep a huge grin from stretching across his face.

He took Lucy-Ann over to the rope again and this time followed up behind her, making sure that she kept her grip.

Outside, Ivan had located the entrance to the gorge and was creeping inside.

The children were now sitting in the cave behind the waterfall and were completely hidden from sight. The rope, still dangling down by the side of the waterfall, was the only clue to their location.

Ivan looked round the gorge then headed towards the rope.

Metres above him, hidden in the cave, Lucy-Ann was towelling her hair dry.

Dinah just sat and gazed at the waterfall as it cascaded past the entrance. "This is such a beautiful place," she said.

"I wish Aunt Allie could see it," said Lucy-Ann.

"So do I," agreed Jack. "But the most important thing is that we're safe,"

"Yeah, for the moment," said Philip.

"Thanks for reminding us, Philip," said Dinah sarcastically.

"Well, there's no point in pretending, is there? We're in a lot of trouble," said Philip seriously. "We're trapped in a valley. There's no way out. And the only company we've got is a maniac who wants to kill us."

"We've got to get that gun," said Jack suddenly.

"We'll have to wait till tomorrow. It'll be dark soon," advised Philip.

"Time for bed! Lights out!" said Kiki.

Jack's stomach let out a sudden rumble that echoed down the tunnel. "I'm starving," he said.

"There's food in my rucksack," said Dinah, producing several bags of crisps and some sandwiches.

"And mine," said Lucy-Ann.

"Get the rope up, will you, Philip?" said Jack, his mouth already full of food.

Below the children, Ivan had just reached the end of the dangling rope. He spat on his hands and prepared to grab the end but, without warning, it jerked away and disappeared above him.

Ivan raised his eyes skyward in exasperation.

He knew that without the rope he'd never make the climb up the side of the waterfall. He didn't even know where the children were, exactly, since he could not see or even hear them talking thanks to the noise of the water falling down.

Hidden in the cave, the four children

were making fast work of the food.

"Tonight, a feast," said Philip. "Then tomorrow, we find the treasure."

CHAPTER TWELVE

When Bill arrived back at Craggy Tops the next morning, he found that Alison had fallen asleep at the kitchen table. He put the kettle on the stove, but before it was even warm Alison had woken up.

"How was the trip to London?" she asked. Bill knew that what she really meant was, "Have you found the children?"

Bill looked grim. "I'll make some tea."

"What is it?" said Alison. "What's the matter?"

Bill paused then said, "Father Paul has disappeared."

"What do you mean, disappeared? You were having him watched," said Alison, now becoming very alarmed.

"I had four men watching his hotel, but late last night he gave them the slip."

"How?"

"In his room they found his priest's robes. He must have had a change of clothes. He'd also shaved off his beard. My men were watching for a priest. He changed into civilian clothes and walked straight past them," explained Bill.

"Oh Bill," said Alison, close to tears.

"I'm sorry. I'm really sorry. But we'll find him, I promise," said Bill, putting a reassuring hand on Alison's shoulder.

The bright light of dawn woke the children early the next morning. They ate the last of their food, then climbed down from the cavern one by one and ventured outside the gorge. They were all excited about seeing the treasure for themselves at last.

"It's been hidden for fifty years," said Jack.

"That's before even Mum was born!" said Dinah to the sound of laughter.

"What if it's not there? What if someone else found it first, years ago?" wondered Philip.

"I hope not," said Jack. "I'd hate to think

all this was for nothing."

As the four children and Kiki set off through the woods, their voices woke up Ivan, who had slept outside the cavern. It was the last place he had seen the children and he was not about to go back to Terry without them. He stayed hidden as they walked by, then quietly began to follow them.

"Right, which way to this bear cave then?" asked Dinah.

"Towards the river first," said Jack, remembering what Otto had told them.

"Lead on, Captain Jack," said Philip.

"It's a shame you can't eat treasure. I'm still starving," added Jack.

"You're always hungry," complained Lucy-Ann.

"Well, you had the last biscuit," said Jack.

"Only because we didn't have a knife to divide it into four," said Lucy-Ann, with a grin.

"Stop it, you two, and get going," ordered Dinah, walking behind them.

The children made their way through

the woods until they found the river, then they followed its twisting path through the valley.

As they were walking, there came a loud buzzing from the sky above them.

"Look, it's Bill's plane!" cried Philip. They all dived for cover as the plane flew over them. It rose sharply, soared out of the valley, and was soon gone.

"I wonder where they're going?" said Jack.

"Terry must be taking it somewhere," said Dinah. "I wonder why."

"Never mind. With them out of the way, this is our chance to find the treasure," said Philip. "How near are we?"

Jack checked his bearings again. "It must be somewhere around this hill. Otto said look for a rock in the shape of a bear, remember," said Jack.

"Let's hope that he's remembered right. It was ages ago," said Lucy-Ann.

"The rock should still be there. Come on! This way," said Jack, heading off.

Behind them Ivan was hiding, listening to their conversation. If he could capture the children and find the treasure Father Paul and Terry would be very pleased.

"Come on, Kiki! Catch up!" shouted Jack, leading the group. Kiki cocked her head, then flew after the children.

"Good morning! Good morning!" she said, landing on Jack's outstretched arm.

"I wish I could fly," said Lucy-Ann. "I'm tired. I hope we find it soon."

When the children reached the top of the hill they began searching for the bear rock. Half an hour later they had still found nothing.

Jack sat down on a large rounded rock, disappointed.

"Are you sure he said a bear?" asked Philip.

"You heard him as well," said Jack defensively.

"Well, there's no bear here," said Dinah. "Maybe we're in the wrong place."

"I'm sure it's round here," said Jack, getting up again. "I'll look over there." He headed up the hill.

"Perhaps the rock has got overgrown with plants and stuff and we can't see it?" said Lucy-Ann.

"Or maybe it rolled away down the hill," said Dinah. "Let's check out the bottom."

The two girls walked down the hill.

"Even if you find it, that won't tell us where the cave is, will it?" shouted Philip after them.

Jack perched on another rock to get his breath back and looked down towards the others. The view seemed to give him an idea.

"Hang on. Maybe Di's right. What if it did roll or maybe broke up? Perhaps we're not looking for one big rock, but two or three pieces," he said, thinking aloud.

"Like a jigsaw?" said Lucy-Ann.

Dinah tilted her head and took another look at the rock in front of her. "Well, what about this?" she said, pointing to a curiously-shaped lump. She ran over to it and started brushing away the earth around it. "I think this is the head!"

"It is! It is!" said Lucy-Ann excitedly.

"So where's the body?" said Jack, looking all around him.

"You're sitting on it!" said Dinah. "Look,

that's the body. The head must have broken off at some point and rolled downhill."

Dinah, Lucy-Ann, and Philip joined Jack on the rock. They climbed down the other side and after a few minutes had found the entrance to a cave.

"This is it!" said Jack. "Got to be."

"The treasure's been lost for fifty years and we're the first ones to find it!" said Dinah. "Excellent!"

Kiki took up her usual position on Jack's shoulder and the four children stepped into the darkened cave.

From his hiding place nearby, Ivan watched the children go inside and smiled to himself. Things were going well.

The dark passage soon opened out into a much larger cavern.

"Wow! It's really big," said Philip, shining his torch around so that they could see as much as possible. The air was dusty and stale. After all, no one had been inside to disturb things for half a century.

"It's a bit creepy," said Lucy-Ann, who only had her tiny pencil torch to light the way.

Kiki let out a sudden screech and went flying across the cavern into the darkness.

As Jack stepped forward he felt his foot press down on some kind of metal plate in the floor. A loud click sounded around the cave.

"What was that?" asked Jack.

"An echo?" said Lucy-Ann, as Jack's words echoed back to them.

"No, before that. The noise," said Jack.

Suddenly the sound was magnified to deafening proportions. It was the metallic rustling of a steel chain unwinding.

"What is it?" screamed Dinah, terrified.

Jack saw something move in the darkness above them.

"Watch out!" Jack dived towards Lucy-Ann and Dinah, pulling them to the floor.

The children looked up to see a wooden object hurtling down at them from the cave roof.

The booby-trap was fifty years old, but the sharp metal spikes and bayonets on it were as deadly as ever.

Jack looked up and saw the spikes

falling straight towards them. He put his arm round Lucy-Ann and closed his eyes.

CHAPTER THIRTEEN

Lucy-Ann let out a scream of terror as the spikes slammed to an abrupt halt just above them. Luckily the booby-trap had been designed for adults at walking height.

Just then, the rusty mechanism suddenly dropped another inch lower, then stopped again.

"Let's get out of here fast!" ordered Philip.

Jack was the first to crawl out from under it. He reached back for Lucy-Ann.

"Give me your hand."

Jack dragged Lucy-Ann with him as Philip and Dinah wriggled frantically away.

"Come on!"

The frame fell to the floor with a massive thud, just missing Dinah's foot.

The children breathed a collective sigh of relief. Jack, though, was angry.

"Otto didn't say anything about booby-traps," he complained.

"Let's hope there aren't any more," said Philip. He led the way into the next tunnel, moving more slowly and much more cautiously than before.

Ivan returned to the cottage after he was certain that the children had gone into the cave. He wasn't sure whether Terry would be back from his expedition to collect Father Paul from the pre-arranged meeting place, but when he opened the door, there they both were. Father Paul saw his nephew straight away and rushed over to him.

"Alexandreyev Dyneisevich!" he said, embracing Ivan.

"Very touching, I'm sure," said Terry to Ivan. "But while you've been waltzing around the woods, something has happened." He held up a severed rope and went on: "When I left in the plane to collect your old uncle here, Otto was all nicely tied up. Snug as a bug. And since you've been gone, he's escaped again," said Terry, angrily.

"It not matter," said Ivan with a grin.

"It flipping matters to me, you great Russian berk. He's gone off to find the treasure, hasn't he?" said Terry.

Ivan raised himself to his full height. "I find treasure," he said proudly.

"What?" said Terry after a slight pause.

"I find treasure by myself. While you gone."

"How?" said Terry. The surprise had reduced him to words of one syllable.

"I follow children through woods. For miles. Watch them solve puzzle. I show you where," said Ivan.

Father Paul gave Ivan a slap on the back and beamed over at Terry, who was speechless.

"We go now," ordered Ivan, leading them out of the cottage. "I show you."

Otto had also found his way to the treasure cave. Luckily he had spotted Ivan hiding outside, and forced himself to wait until he left. Then he had silently followed the children into the darkness. When he saw the booby-trap lying harmlessly on the floor, he let out a sigh of relief. He had completely forgotten it was there.

"You are very lucky children," he smiled to himself, moving carefully round the sharp spears of the trap. Near the far wall he saw an old lantern lying in the gloom and picked it up. He shook it to see whether there was any fuel inside, and could hear a welcome splashing. He took out his pocket lighter and lit the lantern.

"Better to have light," he said, walking on, "to see my treasure."

Much further along the system of tunnels and caverns, the children were still searching for the same treasure.

"How much further?" asked Dinah, who was getting a little fed up.

"Otto and his friends certainly didn't want anybody else to be able to steal it, that's for sure," said Philip.

"Will we get a reward if we find the treasure?" said Lucy-Ann.

"Probably," said Jack. "We certainly

deserve one."

"I know just what I'm going to buy with mine," said Lucy-Ann.

The beam of her small pencil torch suddenly illuminated the empty eye sockets of a skull. Underneath it was the rest of the bare skeleton.

"Aaaah!" she screamed.

"You'd be best off buying a first-class air ticket out of this place," said Jack.

The children walked onwards, moving more quickly now. They turned another corner in the tunnel and found themselves in a man-made cavern.

"Looks like someone dug this deeper section out by hand," said Philip. There were tools and other equipment abandoned all over the floor.

"It must have taken ages," observed Jack. "But why did they do it? Surely there must have been a reason?"

The children shone their torches around. The beam from Philip's torch picked out a massive metal door.

"Look!" said Lucy-Ann. "This must be the door to the treasure trove itself."

There was a bar across the door secured by a huge metal padlock.

"Don't say we've come all this way and we can't get in," groaned Dinah.

Jack looked among the tools and spotted a large sledgehammer. He picked it up. "That lock's so old, maybe we can smash it."

There was a momentous clang as Jack hit the lock.

"They'll hear that back at Craggy Tops!" smiled Lucy-Ann.

"Try it again," encouraged Dinah. "It's almost broken."

Philip took the sledgehammer from Jack and took a powerful swing. The impact of the blow sent the lock falling to the floor.

"Yes! Got it. Well done, Philip!" cried Lucy-Ann.

"Now heave!" said Jack as Philip and Dinah attempted to lift the bar out of position, but it was too heavy and they had to let it fall back into place.

"All together, heave!" repeated Jack. He and Lucy-Ann stepped in to add their help. The bar slowly moved upwards, then fell to the floor.

They were in!

"Open the door! Open the door!" cackled Kiki, flying on to Jack's shoulder.

"Trust you, Kiki,"

"Wipe your feet! Naughty boy!" said Kiki, enjoying herself.

The four children leant against the door and pushed as hard as they could. The rusty hinges had not been moved for fifty years.

The door swung open. Jack pointed his torch inside.

"Gold!" he whispered in awe.

The entire room was full of gold. Gold statues, gold candlesticks, gold chalices – everything was gold. As Jack's torch beam travelled across the treasure, the room itself seemed to gleam and glisten. In the middle of it all Jack's torchlight illuminated the Golden Madonna.

"It's beautiful," said Lucy-Ann.

"It's got to be worth millions," said Philip.

The four children's mouths were open in amazement as they stepped inside to take a closer look.

CHAPTER FOURTEEN

The Land Rover came skidding to a halt outside Craggy Tops. Alison watched from a window as Bill got out and ran to the house.

"Allie, get your coat. I've had an idea. We're leaving."

Bill rushed Alison out of the house. It was not until they were hurtling down the road towards the airfield again that Bill started explaining things.

"I've always said if you want a job done properly, do it yourself. So after Father Paul gave us the slip, I started looking into Otto Scheer's background a little more closely."

Alison closed her eyes as Bill swerved the Land Rover round a bend in the road.

He was in a real hurry.

"What did you find?" said Alison, opening her eyes again.

"I read through some classified war files. I found a map that showed where Otto's plane had crashed after the end of the war, in the foothills of the Black Mountains. Chances are he was on his way back from hiding the treasure," continued Bill.

"How does that help us?" asked Alison.

"If Father Paul wants his Golden Madonna it would make sense for him to take Otto back to where he hid it," Bill explained.

"You think that the children could be in those mountains?" groaned Alison. "It's such a big area."

"I know. But it's the best lead we've got. There'll be a helicopter waiting for us at the airfield," said Bill.

He pushed his foot down on the accelerator and the Land Rover hurtled forwards.

The four children walked around the

treasure cave lighting the hundreds of candles already set up everywhere. The jewelled treasures glittered in the warm golden glow.

"It's like a church," said Dinah.

"Most of this stuff should be in a church," said Philip. "That's where it was stolen from in the first place."

Jack began to hum to himself. He was singing something that sounded like an old Latin psalm.

There was now just one tall candlestick that was not alight. Jack climbed on to a packing case and reached up to it. As he stretched out his arm, he lost his balance and fell heavily to the floor.

"Ow! My ankle!" said Jack.

The others rushed over to him.

"Let me see it," said Dinah, giving it a testing prod.

"Ow! That hurts!"

"It's not broken," said Dinah, feeling Jack's ankle more gently. "It must be strained. Looks like it's swelling up already."

While the children were attending to

Jack, another figure silently entered the room behind them. It was Otto. After fifty years he had finally came face to face with his treasure trove again. He stared in silent admiration.

Across the room, the children were still gathered round Jack. Lucy-Ann spotted something lying abandoned between two packing cases.

"Look! It's the gun," she said, pointing.

Philip leant over and picked it up.

"Will it still work? That's the question," said Dinah.

The children looked down at the old weapon in Philip's hands, wondering what to do next.

"I can make it work," said Otto's voice.

They turned round swiftly to find Otto between them and the door.

"You've done well," he said. "Now, give the gun to me." Philip moved forward to hand it over, but then hesitated. Could they really trust Otto?

"Give the gun to me, boy," said Otto, harshly.

"No! Don't give it to him, Philip! We

don't know what he'll do," said Lucy-Ann.

Otto and the children heard footsteps coming along the tunnel outside. They all knew that it had to be Terry and Ivan.

"They are coming! Quickly, give it to me!" said Otto. "It is our only chance."

Philip handed the gun to Otto just as Terry, Ivan, and Father Paul walked into the room.

The old man spun round awkwardly and turned to point the gun at the new arrivals.

"Put your hands up where I can see them!" said Otto.

Father Paul ignored Otto completely. He fell to his knees in front of the Golden Madonna and crossed himself reverentially.

Terry grinned and slowly raised his own gun until it was pointing straight at Otto.

"You put your hands up!" said Terry.

"I will not hesitate to shoot you," warned Otto.

"With that old thing, Fritz? It'll probably blow up in your face," smiled Terry.

Otto's finger tightened on the trigger of

his weapon. "Do you really want to take that chance, my friend?"

The children stood frozen behind Otto.

Terry's brow broke out in sweat.

"Ah, this is foolish. You don't want the reward, do you?" said Otto. "You really want the treasure for yourself, yes?"

Ivan and Father Paul looked hard at Terry.

"Why should we fight over it," continued Otto, "when there is enough to share?"

"Otto, you said you'd take it all back," said Jack indignantly.

"Silence, boy!" snapped Otto.

Terry put a thoughtful hand on his chin and rubbed it. "I like your style, Fritz. I'll give you that. And you're right, I was going to take the lot myself."

Father Paul and Ivan now realised that Terry had intended to betray them from the very beginning. Full of anger, Ivan suddenly lunged towards Terry. Terry pointed his gun and stopped the big Russian in his tracks.

"Hey, hey, watch it!" said Terry.

"You cannot take all this," said Father Paul, looking round him. "There's too much for you to move."

"You're dead right, Father Paul. That's why I've got a bunch of the lads waiting to ship it out for me," said Terry with no hint of regret.

He looked across at Otto. For a second he seemed to be weighing him up, then he said, "You ready, Fritz?"

"I have been ready for half a century," said Otto.

The thought that Otto might take the Golden Madonna away from him again was too much for Father Paul. He rushed at Otto, who raised the ancient gun.

"Back off! Back off!" said Terry, intervening. "Take it easy with that gun, Fritzie. It might blow us all up. Let's just let them sweat until we get back."

Terry and Otto retreated, keeping their weapons trained on the others. They stepped outside and slammed the heavy metal door shut.

"They can't lock us in!" whispered Lucy-Ann.

Ivan ran towards the door and strained against it, but it was too late. On the other side, Terry and Otto had put the bar back into its locked position.

"There!" said Terry.

"We need to wedge it as well," said Otto.

Terry picked up the sledgehammer and banged a piece of metal under the door to wedge it shut. Otto silently put down the old gun and moved closer behind Terry. He suddenly snatched the gun from Terry's belt.

Terry turned round to find himself looking down the barrel of his own gun.

"A precaution, my friend," said Otto, now in command.

"Why?"

"Perhaps you think you do not need this old fool now?" said Otto, aiming the gun carefully.

"Otto! Hey, we're partners. I'm very hurt," said Terry. Otto looked away for just a second and Terry had the chance to snatch up the old gun. "Now we've both got guns again."

Terry pointed the ancient weapon over Otto's head and pulled the trigger to fire a warning shot. Nothing happened.

"So it is kaput," laughed Otto. He waved Terry's working gun in his face. "Come on, partner. Let's go."

Otto pushed Terry down the tunnel at gunpoint. Behind them, the children were left trapped inside the treasure room.

CHAPTER FIFTEEN

"He has betrayed us!" said Father Paul angrily. "I will not lose the Golden Madonna a second time."

As Terry and Otto's footsteps faded into the distance Father Paul and Ivan began talking in Russian.

The children gathered together to try to work out a plan.

"First, I think we should put some of these candles out, so we make sure they last longer," said Dinah.

Philip found a candle snuffer and passed it to Dinah.

"There's no hope of getting the door open," said Jack. "They must have jammed it shut."

"I wonder how long it'll be before they come back?" said Lucy-Ann.

"I don't know, but I'm not in any hurry for them to return," said Jack, picking up Kiki.

Suddenly the candles that were still left alight flickered violently and a few blew out.

"There's a draught coming in from somewhere," announced Philip.

"I hope it doesn't blow all the candles out," said Lucy-Ann, not understanding his point.

Philip held up a lit candle in front of him and attempted to find where the draught was coming from. "Don't you get it?" he said. "If air can get in, maybe we can get out." He followed the draught until he found a large grille high in the cave wall. "I think it's coming from here," he said.

"Leave it, Philip. It's not worth breaking your leg for," said Dinah irritably.

"This might be our way out," said Philip, trying to open it. He put his ear close to it and listened. "Sshh! I can hear something."

"What is it?" asked Lucy-Ann.

"It's like a rushing sound," answered Philip.

"It's probably the plane taking off again," said Dinah, now very fed up.

"No, they couldn't have got all the way back there yet," said Jack.

"It sounds just like when we were trapped in the tunnel after the rockfall. It sounds like running water. Let's prise this grille open," said Philip.

Ivan had come over to see what the children were doing. He handed Philip a shovel. "I very sorry for everything. This not good," said Ivan, as Philip levered open the grille.

Philip squeezed his shoulders through the hole to have a look. "There's a drop, then water rushing by."

Dinah joined him to have a look.

"Where does it go to?" said Jack.

"I can't see. It's too dark," said Philip.

"It must be going somewhere," said Lucy-Ann. "Maybe outside?"

Jack limped towards the others. "Or another underground cavern, even worse than this."

"How could it be worse than this? I vote that we go," said Dinah, who was warming to the idea of doing something.

"Jack could be right, though," said Philip. "I mean, we don't know what might happen."

Dinah's eyes narrowed. "We do know what will happen if we just stay here and do nothing. Terry's coming back with more men."

"Perhaps if only some of us go? Just in case," offered Lucy-Ann.

"I'll go," said Philip. "It makes sense."

"But not on your own," cautioned Jack.

"I go too," said Ivan.

Philip looked at the size of the opening and back to Ivan. "Sorry, Ivan, but you'd never fit through that. And Jack can't go with his ankle twisted."

"So I'll go with you," volunteered Dinah. "I don't mind."

Philip was not happy with the idea. "No way. We don't have a clue what's down there or where it goes. It might not even be a way out."

Dinah looked him straight in the eye. She wasn't taking no for an answer. "I'm as good a swimmer as you are, Philip. I'm coming with you whether you like it or not."

Philip knew that there was no changing Dinah's mind when she was in this mood.

Ivan handed Philip his torch. "Here, take this. It may help."

Jack handed his rucksack to Dinah. "Be safe," he said simply.

"Let's go," said Philip, hoisting himself up and into the opening.

Dinah followed him and the two of them disappeared into the darkness, leaving Jack and Lucy-Ann as helpless observers.

The two children looked at each other in horror as they heard Dinah let out a scream a long way below. Jack put his arm round Lucy-Ann as the scream tailed off into the distance.

Philip and Dinah found themselves falling along a sharply dipping watershoot. Philip turned on his torch and shone it upwards. They were travelling down a small tunnel half filled with gushing water. The bottom of the tunnel had been eroded by the water, making it smooth and slippery.

The children hurtled down it, gaining speed all the time.

"Put your arms out and try to slow down a bit," shouted Philip, as he took his own advice.

But Philip's left hand caught on something on the wall of the tunnel and he spun round uncontrollably. He tried and failed to find something to grab hold of, then gradually the spin slowed and he began to enjoy the ride.

"Back home you'd have to go to a theme park and pay for this," he shouted.

Dinah let out another scream of part terror and part excitement as the water hurled them both along like driftwood.

"I hope there's a safety net to stop us at the end!" she shouted back to him.

The noise of the rushing water had now increased to a roar.

"I can see light," called Philip, but before Dinah had a chance to answer they shot out of the tunnel through a large fissure in the rock wall and sailed through the air. Philip looked down and saw with relief that underneath them was a deep pool of clear mountain water.

They splash-landed and disappeared underwater. Dinah was the first to resurface. She anxiously looked around for Philip, but couldn't see him anywhere. Suddenly he broke the surface as well, breathless but smiling.

"Some theme park ride!" he grinned. "Come on, let's get out of here."

CHAPTER SIXTEEN

Otto led Terry out of the cave and past the broken bits of the bear rock.

"Look, Otto, mate. I could get there twice as fast on my own," said Terry, who was desperate for an excuse to get away.

"We go together, partner," said Otto, firmly dismissing the idea.

They headed down the hill and then tracked along the river and through the forest.

"Wait," said Otto finally. He was exhausted and had to lean against a tree.

"We're never gonna get there at this flipping rate," said Terry. "Not unless I carry you," he said ironically.

Otto's eyes suddenly lit up.

A few hundred metres further away,

Philip and Dinah were also making their way through the woods. They too were heading towards the old cottage and the plane.

"I've got to get on that plane. It's the only way we can get out of the valley and get help," said Philip.

"We'll both go," volunteered Dinah.

"No, it's too risky in daylight. And if I get caught, at least you'll have a chance of freeing the others," said Philip, handing her Ivan's torch.

"*Schnell!*" came a voice through the trees.

"That sounds like Otto. Get down," said Philip.

The two children ducked down into the undergrowth as Otto appeared masterfully riding Terry piggy-back. Terry looked like he was regretting having the idea already.

"*Schnell! Schnell!*" commanded Otto, waving the gun like a horse whip.

Philip and Dinah watched in amazement as the horse and rider disappeared through the trees.

"They're going to get to the plane before

us," cried Dinah.

Philip thought quickly. "We need something to distract their attention," he said.

Dinah opened her rucksack and looked inside. "The flares!" she said.

"Come on! We'll have to run!" ordered Philip.

Inside the treasure cave, Father Paul sat lost in thought. He was not a happy man. His plan to retrieve the Golden Madonna had gone horribly wrong. Even worse, he had endangered the four children. And, as Jack reminded him, a parrot.

"Your friends are very brave," said Father Paul, breaking the grim silence.

"I should have gone, not Dinah," said Jack, who was more than a little frustrated at just sitting around.

"You couldn't. Your ankle," said Lucy-Ann.

"I could have tried. It's only a strain," said Jack.

"Do you think we should follow them?" asked Lucy-Ann, climbing up and looking through the open grille into the darkness.

"No," said Jack. "Better not. We don't know what's happened to them, do we?"

Jack looked at Lucy-Ann and saw in her eyes how worried she was about Philip and Dinah.

"Cheer up, Lucy-Ann. I'm sure they're OK," he said.

Ivan, who had been stroking Kiki, suddenly stepped forward. "Sing," he said.

"Pardon?" The children were baffled by this strange command.

"In Russia, we sing when we are sad," said Ivan, sitting down next to Lucy-Ann.

"Would you like him to teach you?" asked Father Paul.

"Oh yes, please," said Lucy-Ann. At that moment any distraction was very welcome.

Ivan launched into a Russian song, followed by Father Paul. Jack and Lucy-Ann joined in as best they could. Soon even Kiki was moving her head in time with the rhythm.

Philip and Dinah saw the plane by the

cottage, where it had been before. They ran through the woods as fast as they could go without making too much noise, splitting up when they got near the landing field.

Dinah waited at the edge of the woods while Philip moved into position behind the plane. He started his run towards the plane just as Otto came out of the woods, riding Terry.

Philip made it safely to the far side of the plane without them seeing, but the two men were now between him and the plane door. He couldn't get on board without them seeing him.

"You wait!" said Terry, as Otto got off his back. Terry was sweating and exhausted. "I'll get you for this, Fritz!"

Philip paused nervously, hidden on the other side of the plane only feet away from the men.

"Come on, Di," he whispered to himself anxiously.

There was a sudden whooshing sound from the hillside. Otto and Terry turned to look in that direction as a bright red distress flare exploded high in the sky.

While their attention was on the flare, Philip crept towards the door of the plane and climbed quietly inside.

"*Donner und blitzen!*" said Otto quietly, eyes still focused on the dying red flare.

"There must be more of them," said Terry urgently. "They're signalling to someone."

The two men boarded the plane and Terry quickly started the engine. Safely hidden behind the rear seats was Philip.

Dinah watched as the plane revved up and then sped along the field. It took off and rose quickly towards the surrounding mountains. She stood up and headed back through the woods towards the treasure cave.

The Land Rover pulled up next to the control tower of Ashburnham airfield. As Bill and Alison got out, an officer in full military uniform came over and saluted Bill.

"Good to see you again, Ron," said Bill, saluting also, then shaking his hand. "Thanks for meeting us here."

He turned to introduce Alison. "Ron, this is Alison Mannering, the mother of two of the children. Alison, this is an old friend of mine, Major Ron Oultram."

"Pleased to meet you, Mrs Mannering. Bill's always talking about you," said the Major. Bill looked a little awkward. "I'm only sorry we had to meet under these circumstances," finished the Major.

"Thank you," said Alison.

"Is everything set up?" asked Bill, as they walked towards the helicopter. Three soldiers were waiting for them by the side of it.

"Everything's ready now. Do you know where you're going?" said the Major.

"Like I told you, somewhere in the Black Mountains," said Bill. "I know it's a big area, but right now it's all we've got."

"Well, our best navigator is on board waiting for you. There's nothing he doesn't know about the area," said the Major.

"Thanks for all your help. It's appreciated," said Bill, helping Alison inside the helicopter. The three armed soldiers climbed inside after them and took the rear seats.

"Good luck," shouted Major Oultram. He said something else, but it was lost in the enormous noise of the rotor blades coming to life.

The helicopter jerked into the air and rose at an alarming rate. Alison felt as if she'd left her stomach somewhere on the ground.

"Come on, Allie," said Bill, giving her hand a squeeze. "Let's go and find those kids."

CHAPTER SEVENTEEN

Terry flew for about an hour before he and Otto brought their plane down on a small landing strip. Waiting for them on the tarmac was a van with Terry's hired helpers. Otto followed Terry out of the plane.

"Remember, my friend, I am only one bullet behind you," he threatened him as they walked towards the men.

Philip popped his head up and peered out of the plane window. Terry and Otto were busy trying to organise the men and the equipment. Philip opened the aircraft door and slipped out unseen. As he made his escape he could hear Terry shouting at the men.

"*Guten Tag*, lads," said Terry, exercising his limited German. "Nice timing. No, not that," he said, pointing to some items they weren't going to need, and making them load numerous different-sized boxes. "*Nein, nein*, you *Dummkopf*. Take that and this. *Schnell! Schnell!*" he went on, trying to hurry them up.

Philip got away from the airstrip as fast as he could. He crossed a muddy field and found a small track. He headed along it towards what looked like a motorway in the extreme distance.

On the right-hand side of the track he passed a small garage, but it was locked up and deserted. There was no one there to help him. But as Philip got nearer the motorway, he caught sight of a German policeman on a motorbike. He waved his arms furiously to get his attention.

"Hey! Hey!" Philip shouted, running towards him. "Hey, stop!" The policeman saw Philip and pulled up.

Bill's helicopter was in the air over Germany, closing in on the Black Mountains. Bill was sitting at the front next to the pilot and was studying the map of

Otto's original crash site.

A message came over the pilot's headset and he turned to Bill.

"Sir, put on your headset. There's a phone call for you. Major Oultram at Ground Control has had it patched straight through," said the pilot.

Bill slid the headset on. "This is Bill Cunningham. Go ahead."

"Uncle Bill?" said a voice over the static. "It's me, Philip!"

Meanwhile, Dinah had trekked all the way back to the entrance by the bear rock. She ran down the tunnel towards the cave and banged the door with her hand, but she couldn't make herself heard above the noise of their singing.

"Jack! Lucy-Ann!"

There was no answer. Dinah saw that the door was wedged shut with a piece of metal. She tried to pull it out, but it was impossible to move.

"Where's that hammer?" she said to herself, looking round. She found it, but it took all her strength just to lift it.

She carried it to the door and managed to strike a blow at the wedge. The loud clang echoed through the treasure room and there was a sudden silence as everyone stopped singing.

"What's that noise?" asked Lucy-Ann. They approached the door slowly, worried that Terry and Otto might have returned.

"Who's there?" shouted Jack through the door.

"Jack? It's me, Dinah!" she called back.

Inside, Jack started to push against the door, hoping to help Dinah. However, the pushing only wedged the door tighter shut.

"Don't push!" shouted Dinah, but by now everyone inside had joined in and they were all pushing against the door.

Finally a small crack opened enough for Dinah to tell them to stop. She summoned her last energy and aimed one final blow at the wedge. It was knocked out of position and the door burst open.

Jack emerged, followed by Lucy-Ann. Dinah was more than happy to see them both and began to speak, but Jack's face stopped her.

"Oh dear! Oh dear!" said Kiki, from her perch on his shoulder.

Dinah looked round. Coming down the tunnel towards them were Otto, Terry and all his men.

"Greetings, my friends," said Otto. "I hope you have been looking after my treasure, yes?"

Otto herded the three children, Ivan and Father Paul into a corner of the cave. Terry supervised his men as they set about packing the treasure into crates. He watched with a big grin on his face until one of the men banged a small statue on the edge of a wooden box.

"Careful with that, you great oaf!" shouted Terry. "That's not off some market stall down the Mile End Road, you know."

The packing went on for quite a while.

"Come here and make yourself useful, Boris," said Terry to Ivan. He pointed to the Golden Madonna.

Ivan carefully took the statue in his arms. The sight of the Golden Madonna being moved was too much for Father

Paul. He rushed at Terry, hitting out at him.

"Get away!" said Otto, pointing his gun.

Ivan put down the Golden Madonna.

"*Niet*. No. I will not let you take her away again," said Father Paul, standing in front of the statue.

"Then I'll do what I should have done years ago," said Otto, raising his gun to fire at the priest.

"Don't shoot him, you coward!" shouted Jack.

Lucy-Ann rushed at Otto. "Stop!" she joined in.

Otto pushed her aside and aimed his gun again, but before he could fire there came the sound of more footsteps in the tunnel. Otto glanced round in astonishment.

Bill and the three soldiers rushed into the cave with their weapons at the ready. Philip followed just behind them.

"Drop your weapons! Nobody move!" shouted Bill.

Lucy-Ann was delighted to see him. "Uncle Bill!" she cried.

Otto quickly sized up the situation and

realised that the odds were now heavily stacked against him. He moved behind Jack, Lucy-Ann, and Dinah, using them as both a shield and as hostages.

"Drop your weapons, or I fire," said Otto coldly.

Bill and his men froze, then slowly lowered their guns. They had no choice. Bill reluctantly let his gun drop to the floor. The soldiers followed his lead.

Father Paul watched Otto from his position by the side of the Golden Madonna.

Terry leant down to pick up a gun.

"Stop!" ordered Otto, including Terry in the range of his gunfire. "Our partnership has outlived its usefulness."

"But Otto—" pleaded Terry.

"What happened to 'Fritzie'?" sneered Otto, thinking back to all Terry's insults.

"You won't get away with this," said Terry desperately.

"Why not?" asked Otto. "These men will pack up the treasure for me – they will work for anyone who pays them," he continued. "The rest of you, say your goodbyes."

At that moment, above him, the Golden Madonna rocked a little on her perch. Suddenly she toppled from where she stood. Perhaps she had a little help from Father Paul, perhaps she didn't. No one saw exactly what happened.

"Look out!" called Terry, but it was too late. The priceless statue crashed down on Otto, dealing him a glancing blow to the head.

Otto fell to the floor and dropped his gun.

Before anyone else could react, Bill and his men snatched up their own weapons.

"Nobody move!" ordered Bill for the second time.

Terry made a dash for the door, but found his way blocked by Ivan.

Ivan put a hand on Terry's shoulder and landed a jaw-breaking punch on his chin. Terry fell unconscious to the floor.

"Is not 'Boris'. Is Ivan!" said Ivan to his long-time tormentor.

"Lights out! Lights out!" said Kiki, fluttering over Terry's unconscious body.

The children laughed as Kiki landed on his head.

A few hours later, the children, Alison and Bill were safely back at Craggy Tops.

On their way inside Alison picked up the post.

"There's a letter for you, Philip," she said, handing it over. "Anyone want anything to drink? Who's for a cup of tea?"

"I'd love a hot chocolate," said Lucy-Ann.

A chorus of agreement went up for hot chocolates all round.

Philip opened his letter.

"What is it?" asked Dinah.

"Looks like a holiday brochure," said Philip.

"Kiss me quick! Kiss me quick!" said Kiki, who was sitting on Philip's shoulder.

Philip read from the brochure. "'Experience the thrill of adventure... Go potholing in North Wales. Explore the subterranean tunnels. Discover the breathtaking caves...'"

"Oh no!" they all groaned.

Dinah took the brochure from him.

"'Fly with Terry Small's Airlines,'" she said, looking at the last page.

"What! Does it really say that?" demanded Jack.

The children crowded round for a closer look.

"Don't be silly," said Dinah, breaking into a smile. "Of course it doesn't!"

They laughed and trooped out towards the kitchen in search of food and hot chocolate.

The Enid Blyton™ Adventure Series

All eight screenplay novelisations from the Channel 5 series are available from bookshops or, to order direct from the publishers, just make a list of the titles you want and send it with your name and address to:

Dept 6,
HarperCollins*Publishers* Ltd,
Westerhill Road,
Bishopbriggs,
Glasgow G64 2QT

Please enclose a cheque or postal order to the value of the cover price (currently £3.50) plus:

UK and BFPO: Add £1 for the first book, and 25p per copy for each additional book ordered.

Overseas and Eire: Add £2.95 service charge. Books will be sent by surface mail, but quotes for airmail dispatch will be given on request.

A 24-hour telephone ordering service is available to Visa and Access card holders on 0141-772 2281.